YOUNG PLATO AND THE CAVE

BY Γ.Δ. CHEKKΦ © 2014

ILLUSTRATED BY
F·A· CHEKKI

DEDICATION: FOR MY GRANDMOTHER

"EMPLOY YOUR TIME IN IMPROVING YOURSELF BY OTHER MENS WRITINGS, SO THAT YOU SHALL GAIN EASILY WHAT OTHERS HAVE LABORED HARD FOR."

- SOCRATES

"ANY ONE WHO HAS COMMON SENSE WILL REMEMBER THAT THE BEWILDERMENTS OF THE EYES ARE OF TWO KINDS, AND ARISE FROM TWO CAUSES, EITHER FROM COMING OUT OF THE LIGHT OR FROM GOING INTO THE LIGHT."

– PLATO, THE ALLEGORY OF THE CAVE

FORWARD BY THE AUTHOR

Why write about Plato? Why now? Well, during my first semester in college as a pre-law major I had my first political science course, which was Political Philosophy. The astute professor assigned Plato's *The Republic*. And I can still remember our weekly group discussions. The one in particular that stood out to me the most, and that I think about often, was when we discussed *The Allegory of the Cave*. This was a quite strange and mysterious part of the greater work we were studying. Think about it: there is a prison, more or less, with people restrained who live in a cave all of their lives, and the only world they knew was through a shadow-kind-of "puppet show." We do not know who the "shadow-master" is. Then, one day, one of these prisoners escapes. He sees the "real world" outside, and then he goes back to the cave to tell the rest. I suggest reading the entire allegory as it is a wonderfully thought provoking work.

Plato, as both philosopher and historical figure, is *essential* to know. His contributions to the world in terms of science, history, ethics, philosophy, and education are some of the most important and lasting. One can hardly escape at least learning something about Plato, his works or influence. Indeed, his life's work and his legacy are unmistakably evident in Western civilization.

I have toyed around in my head, for some time, with a work concerning Plato and his famous allegory. So, I felt compelled to create *Young Plato and the Cave*, especially with a focus on a youthful audience. As when we are in school learning, reading, engaging in study, said allegory has great value in edifying growing minds in the importance of education or the lack thereof. Yet, there is more to the mystery contained in Plato's work. There is the age old question of *what are the universal truths concerning our reality?*

You will see here in these pages that there is a "literary deviation" from what is known about Plato through what can be learned from the texts available. The story of young Plato's quest for truth involves visiting an Oracle who lives in a chasm. Hence, this is my coloration in the form of fiction and parody. It would be my great pleasure to write and illustrate a story that motivates readers to pick up and read *The Republic* as well as to read about Plato himself. Thus, as a final note, one cannot overestimate or overstress the importance of reading. Yes! Read, read, read! This activity is the exercise for the mind just like sports and fitness are exercise for the body. You will thank yourself for doing it and so will your community and society.

 INTRODUCTION:

A young Plato is with his teacher Socrates one night
in ancient Greece, over 2000 years ago. Sitting around a
fire the great teacher ended his lesson and began to tell a
most fantastic tale.

GREEK KNOWLEDGE - BITE
THE GREAT PHILOSOPHER SOCRATES

Φ Bust of Socrates. Naples, Museo Nazionale.

The great philosopher Socrates was born in 469 B.C. in Greece. He died in 399 B.C. in his hometown, Athens. He is known as one of the greatest philosophers who ever lived. A philosopher is someone who helps us to understand our world: where we came from, where we are now, and where we are going in the future. Arrested and tried by his people for "corrupting the youth" with his teachings and philosophy, Socrates' sentence was to choose between death by poisoning or exile. Out of his convictions and out of protest, he chose death. He drank hemlock and died close beside his disciples. For in exile, Socrates would not have been true to himself. Today, we question why the philosopher was treated so harsh. Socrates is now heralded as a true hero for standing up for what he believed.

 There once was a young man named Plato who lived in the far off past.
And there was a wise man named Socrates whose teachings did ever last.

"Open your mind and empty your thoughts," he told the young Plato.
"I'll tell you of a mysterious, dark, cave where in my youth I then did go."

GREEK KNOWLEDGE - BITE 𝖎𝖎
THE ALLEGORY OF THE CAVE

Φ   Allegory of the cave Jan Saenredam (1565–1607) After Cornelis Cornelisz van Haarlem (1562–1638) Plato's Allegory of the cave 1604 engraving.

It would be Plato, in his later years, who would write an important work known as *The Republic*.   Plato, like Socrates, became a philosopher. He also wrote a famous story, which is so much more than just a story, called an allegory. It can be found in the aforementioned work. This story has become known as *The Allegory of the Cave*. An allegory is a story that has meaning beyond what the story is literally about. One meaning in this particular allegory surrounds the importance of education for everyone and the implication of the lack of education.

 To Socrates, Plato asked, "Where is this strange cave? Why the mystery?"
Replied he, "The cave lies beyond your home, and is well beyond our city.

There is an Oracle there who will tell you more, and you will see 'the light.'
She will reveal a truth I learned of as a boy and will not tell of now this night."

GREEK KNOWLEDGE – BITE II
THE CITY-STATE OF ATHENS, GREECE

Φ The Acropolis of Athens by Leo von Klenze (1846).

In ancient Greece, nations were divided into what are called "city-states." These are cities that encompass an entire country of people, and Greece was made up of many city-states. One of the greatest was Athens. Athenians lived here and still do. Athens was one of the greatest city-states because of its culture, economy, art, architecture, and its philosophers, among other things of course (508–322 B.C.). This place was home to Socrates and Plato. Some of its remarkable buildings, now ruins such as the Acropolis, can be seen there to this day. Athens was a renowned center of learning and sharing knowledge.

 Socrates' tale left Plato pondering, curious; all night the cave was on his mind. So the next day he made his way to the mountains to see what he would find.

The sun beat down and the day was long, but Plato carried on in wonderment. For what he would discover yonder and far kept up his march and merriment.

III.

GREEK KNOWLEDGE - BITE
MOUNT OLYMPUS

Φ   Hercules ex rogo in polum.: [Hercules, led by Jupiter, goes to Mount Olympus to live with the gods after burning his mortal body on a funeral pyre.] Baur, Joh. Wilhelm (Johann Wilhelm), 1600-1642 -- Artist.

One of the most famous mountains in the world is Mount Olympus, situated in Greece. During ancient times, this mountain had important significance in Greek society. In Greek mythology it is believed to be the home of the 12 Olympian gods. It is the setting of many ancient Greek stories. While not one of the tallest mountains in the world, Mount Olympus is one of the most beautiful sites in modern day Greece. It was likewise so in ancient Greece. Due to its beauty, it was a fitting place for the home of the gods.

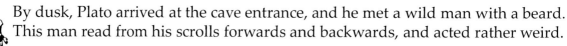 By dusk, Plato arrived at the cave entrance, and he met a wild man with a beard. This man read from his scrolls forwards and backwards, and acted rather weird.

Within the cave he said he once did live, once shadowed in the dark, in his youth. He said that when he left "I tried to live like you, but could not because of *Truth*."

GREEK KNOWLEDGE - BITE ▥
THE GREAT LIBRARY OF ALEXANDRIA

Φ   Alexandria Fire by Hermann Goll (1876).

The ancient Greek people were productive writers, thinkers, and scholars. They kept many writings. Perhaps the greatest of all libraries was once the Library of Alexandria, which flourished at the height of Greek power (323–283 B.C.). It contained more writings than any other libraries of the period and it was home to the recordings of some of humankind's greatest achievements at the time. It was, unfortunately, burned down during successive wars and military conquests. While some of the works may have been lost in the fires, it is believed many were saved and kept in various libraries throughout the Western world.

 As Plato approached this stranger babbled, "Enter lad, if you so shall dare. *Go in*! *In, go!* When you leave you'll *never be the same*." He said, with a stare.

The free and feral man then sang to himself - and puttered off - out of tune. Plato, determined, continued and entered the cave, thinking: *What a buffoon!*

V.

GREEK KNOWLEDGE - BITE
EDUCATION IN ANCIENT GREECE

Φ Raphael, The School of Athens (1509-1510).

Education was a very important part of ancient Greek life. Children were taught to first count and to draw. Following, they were taught their letters and syllables, then words and sentences, reading and writing. Eventually, children were given poetry to read, memorize, and recite. Physical education was also a part of a child's education. The focus of ancient Greek education was to develop body, mind, and imagination. In many ways, these are still an integral part of modern elementary education.

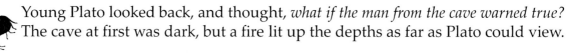 Young Plato looked back, and thought, *what if the man from the cave warned true?*
The cave at first was dark, but a fire lit up the depths as far as Plato could view.

Remembering then an Oracle dwell within the cave, he traveled lower to her lair.
Feeling nothing to fear Plato voyaged onward as if there was no time left to spare.

VI.

GREEK KNOWLEDGE - BITE II
THE ORACLE OF DELPHI

Φ The Delphic Orcle. Kylix by the Kodros painter, c. 440-430 B.C. From the Collection of Joan Cadden.

Located at Mount Parnassas, there is a chasm where the Oracle of Delphi could once be found. A female individual, known as the Oracle, was appointed to remain in the chasm to prophesy – to predict the future. The ancient Greeks placed tremendous religious significance on the Oracle and her ability to convey divine messages and to therefore be a voice for the gods. Discovered around 1400 B.C., and up to around 400 A.D., the location would be a place many would take a pilgrimage to in order to have the future told. Greek history may have been shaped in part as a result of some of the prophesies told at Delphi.

 To his amazement, to his inquiry, the young Plato found the Oracle in a hurry. She seemed to be gazing into a water-filled terracotta that was full and dreary.

Yet, the Oracle was blind, blind but she could see! A vision she then did tell: "Past and present, present and past, and a future so far off, I can see as well."

VII.

GREEK KNOWLEDGE - BITE II
THE GREEK NOTION OF ARETE

Φ Statue of Arete in Celsus' Library in Ephesus.

In Greek, *Arete* means "excellence of any kind." This notion, held as part of the ancient Greeks' value system, means one should live life to one's full potential. Moreover, it is the attainment of knowledge which is a substantial element of *Arete*, if not the greatest potential one can achieve.

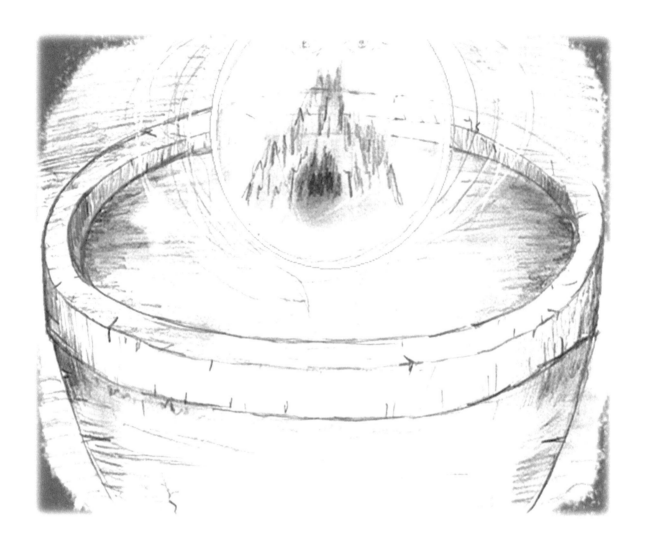

 An orb emerged and from within it revealed a site untoward this place!
Behold! In this cave there once did dwell cruel rulers and an ancient race.

The Oracle had begun to speak, "You fool! You had to know and to pry!
Now I shall show you things: the who, the what, the where, and why."

VIII.

GREEK KNOWLEDGE - BITE II
ANCIENT GREEK ARCHITECTURE - THE PARTHENON

Φ Parthenon, Frederic Edwin Church (1869).

The ancient Greeks are well known for their amazing architecture. Some ruins of important ancient Greek buildings still stand today and are visited by many every year. One such building is the Parthenon (447 B.C. – 432 B.C.). This building is one of the most notable structures from Classical Greece. It was dedicated to the Greek goddess Athena. She was once the patron deity of Athens. Not only is the Parthenon a symbol of ancient Greece, it symbolizes Greek democracy and the great cultural accomplishments of Western civilization.

 "In days long past," the Oracle boldly told, "these cave dwellers were *bound*. That is, they were shackled, with heads braced they could not turn around.

Hence, all were forced to stare upon the shadowy wall; this was their reality. They knew not 'the entirety.' These shadows were their world and society."

GREEK KNOWLEDGE - BITE
ANCIENT GREEK TECHNOLOGY - THE ANTIKYTHERA MECHANISM

Φ http://en.wikipedia.org/wiki/Antikythera_mechanism le images

Found in an old shipwreck (1900-1901 A.D.) off the Greek island of Antikythera, there was submersed a mysterious artifact. It came to be known as the Antikythera Mechanism. Amazingly, this is the earliest known computer. This device was an enigma until the 1970's, after the invention of the modern day computer. What is most incredible about this device was its purpose and its age. It is estimated to have been created around 100 - 87 B.C.! Scientists who have researched and studied the device have determined it was used to calculate the position of the stars and planets, our sun and moon. We do not know of any like-devices prior to the 14th century that are this complex and engineered this well.

 "But there would be one," the Oracle went on, "one man who would leave.
He did proceed outside the cave, and saw a world he could hardly believe.

Once his eyes adjusted to the light of the sun the man realized what was a lie.
As the shadows in the cave that did belie left this wanderer to wonder, *Why*?"

Φ Theatrical masks of Tragedy and Comedy. Mosaic, Roman artwork, 2nd century CE. From the Baths of Decius on the Aventine Hill, Rome.

Much like today, the ancient Greeks and their contemporaries loved theatre as a form of art and entertainment. The ancient Greeks are famous for their plays, one of which is *Oedipus Rex*. This play is still performed in the present. As a part of the theatrics, the actors would wear masks. The masks were a representation of the characters being played. The Greeks used large outside theatres cut into the sides of hills and mountains, called amphitheatres. One can still visit many sites in and around modern day Greece and see these truly marvelous outdoor theatres where ancient Greeks performed many plays. Greek plays are divided into comedies and tragedies.

 "What did he do next?" Plato pled to this teller. She continued and explained: "Upon seeing the truth the man returned to the cave to tell those who remained.

He yelled and screamed what he saw beyond this dark and shadowy abyss. Yet those still inside shunned him and his words, uttering *'What ignorance!'*"

GREEK KNOWLEDGE - BITE III
ANCIENT GREEK RELIGION - THE GODS

Φ Peter Paul Rubens, Neptune Calming the Tempest, (1635).

Ancient Greek life in many ways surrounded the religion and mythology of the times, referred to as polytheism. Instead of having one God - monotheism - as in the predominant Western religions of today, the Greeks believed in a pantheon of gods. The gods were ruled by the greatest, which was Zeus. As depicted in the artwork above, Neptune was the god of the sea. Greeks often called upon their gods for specific requests. Such as with sailing the waters of the Mediterranean Sea, they would pray to Neptune to calm dangerous waters. They would do the same for many reasons; for example farming, war, and even the popular drink of the time which was wine.

 A vision the Oracle would show Plato next, the youth knew not what to think. Foretold, there is this odd *box*, people would watch, with lights that did blink.

And this *box* made sounds, it would astound! A play, a show, right in the home! *What's this magic?* Plato puzzled in his head as his mind then restlessly did roam.

XII

GREEK KNOWLEDGE - BITE II
GREECE - PENINSULA AND ARCHIPELAGO

Φ   19ᵗʰ Century map of Greece: Graecia Antiqua. (with) Graeciae (laxe sumptae) partes boreales compendiose propter amplioris cognitianis peruriam tractalae. Auctore D'Anville. W. Sim, sc, New York. (1814?) .

Ancient Greece was not a unified nation as it is in modern times. Today the nation is classified as a peninsula with an archipelago. This is because the mainland branches from the north into the Mediterranean Sea and has many islands throughout the waters that belong to the nation of Greece, thus comprising the Greek archipelago. The country resides east of Italy and west of Turkey. It is therefore a crossroads to the Middle-East, and has been for many centuries. Rich in old traditions, art and architecture, culture, food and agriculture, trade and tourism, Greece is considered one of the most popular places to visit in all of Europe.

 Further forth in the future the Oracle could *see,* and to Plato she would tell. "These boxes become more mesmerizing where these people then do dwell.

But eventually, it will seem, these people magically lived by *the boxes* you see. They could take these devices wherever they went to, and lived on 'happily.'"

GREEK KNOWLEDGE - BITE II
ANCIENT GREEK ART

Φ Exekias black-figure vase showing Achilles and Ajax playing checkers (540 B.C.).

One of the hallmarks of ancient Greece is its art. The Greeks created many sculptures, paintings, ornate buildings, and of course, pottery. Pottery in ancient Greece was both functional and aesthetic, or artistic. Pottery was used to store food and wine as well as to decorate the Greeks' homes. Pottery often depicted scenes of everyday life in Greece and the Greek gods. The works of Exekias exemplify the achievements in ancient pottery art and techniques.

 "Stupendous! Yes. But quite sad, because for in time the *boxes* become all they know. There were no more writings, no more books read, or libraries where one could go."

"What about the present, what about now?" Plato pried. "It is outside," said she. "Go young Plato, outside the cave; you'll see. Go to be who you are meant to be."

GREEK KNOWLEDGE - BITE 𝕀𝕀
GREEK GOVERNMENT - DEMOCRACY

Φ The Age of Pericles, by Philipp Von Foltz. (1853).

Ancient Greece, particularly Athens, is well known for being home to one of the first successful democratic governments. Although ancient Greek democracy is much different than modern democracy, the ancient Greeks are recognized for having influenced Roman democracy as well as the democracies of the United States, Europe, and other parts of the world. Democracy is a form of government where the people, citizens, vote to make laws and decisions affecting and governing their society. This form of government is yet another lasting influence of the ancient Greeks.

 Plato ascended out and retreated beyond the cave to return upon the early dawn.
He thought about all he saw and what the Oracle said, and looked to the horizon.

Then, the present became clear, and it presented itself to Plato as he traipsed on.
A path home he did follow; yet *his path* indeed t'was a gift toward *truth e'er drawn.*

XV.

GREEK KNOWLEDGE - BITE
THE GREAT PHILOSOPHER PLATO

Φ Plato, Classical bust (Image in public domain).

In all of history, Plato is also one of the most important thinkers, writers, mathematicians, and philosophers. He lived in Athens during the time of Socrates (428 B.C. – 348 B.C.). Socrates was his teacher and mentor, and Plato was in turn teacher and mentor to another most famous of all philosophers, Aristotle. Plato founded the *Academy* in Athens, advancing education in his community. He wrote numerous philosophical dialogues and other writings. He is credited for laying the foundations for Western science, and he is one of the founding fathers of the discipline of philosophy. Plato's contributions to the world are among some of the most noble ever known.

 FIN